TIMBERWOLF Trap

Sigmund Brouwer

illustrated by Dean Griffiths

ORCA BOOK PUBLISHERS

To Micky,
A great kid with a great idea. Thanks!
Remember to chase your dreams.

Library and Archives Canada Cataloguing in Publication

Brouwer, Sigmund, 1959-
Timberwolf trap / written by Sigmund Brouwer ; illustrated by Dean Griffiths.
(Orca echoes)

ISBN 978-1-55143-722-4

I. Griffiths, Dean, 1967- II. Title. III. Series.
PS8553.R68467T548 2007   JC813'.54   C2007-903954-5

First published in the United States, 2007
Library of Congress Control Number: 2007930921

Summary: In this fourth book in the Timberwolves series, Johnny Maverick
and Tom Morgan are in a race for the league's goal-scoring trophy.

Mixed Sources
Product group from well-managed forests,
controlled sources and recycled wood or fiber
www.fsc.org Cert no. SW-COC-000952
© 1996 Forest Stewardship Council
FSC

Orca Book Publishers is dedicated to preserving the environment and has printed this book
on paper certified by the Forest Stewardship Council.

Orca Book Publishers gratefully acknowledges the support for its publishing programs
provided by the following agencies: the Government of Canada through the Canada Book
Fund and the Canada Council for the Arts, and the Province of British Columbia through
the BC Arts Council and the Book Publishing Tax Credit.

Typesetting by Teresa Bubela
Cover artwork and interior illustrations by Dean Griffiths

ORCA BOOK PUBLISHERS   ORCA BOOK PUBLISHERS
PO Box 5626, Stn. B   PO Box 468
Victoria, BC Canada   Custer, WA USA
v8R 6s4   98240-0468

www.orcabook.com
Printed and bound in Canada.

13 12 11 10 • 5 4 3 2

Contents

Stinky was a slow fat dog that hung around the rink. Stinky made loud rude noises that did not come from his front end. Getting stuck in a closet with Stinky was not good, at least not if you liked breathing. Eldridge knew that now.

"You heard about that?" Johnny asked. He wondered if he should try to tell his Dad it had been an accident.

"Don't try to tell me it was an accident," Dad said.

"Of course not," Johnny said.

"You stomped shaving cream on that woman in the hotel during the tournament in Calgary,"[2] Dad said.

"Hey!" Johnny said. He wondered how his dad knew all these things. "It really was an accident! I was trying to get Tom. That woman got in the way."

"You like to mess with your friends," Dad said. "This is perfect because people know I do too. Especially because this is also a secret mission to be a good neighbor. I want to help him build his garage."

---

2. You can find this story in *Timberwolf Revenge*.

Coach Smith was their neighbor. He lived two houses down from Johnny.

"Sneaking gas into Coach Smith's tank makes us good neighbors?" Johnny asked.

"Only a little gas at a time," Dad answered. "Not enough for him to notice on his fuel gauge."

"How does that make us good neighbors?" Johnny asked.

Dad shook his head sadly. "Remember how Coach Smith wouldn't let anyone help him build his deck last spring?"

"He nailed his thumb to a post with the nail gun," Johnny said. Everyone in the neighborhood had been gone that day. Coach Smith had been stuck to the post for two hours. "The deck was crooked and fell apart in the summer when everyone stood on it during his birthday party."

"Some people are too proud to let anyone help," Dad said, "but if he builds the garage by himself, he could get hurt again."

"If the garage falls on someone," Johnny said, "that would be worse than when we fell through his deck."

"Right," Dad said. "That's why Coach Smith's wife gave me a spare key to his car."

"She knows about this too?" Johnny said. "I don't understand what is going on."

"You will." Dad grinned at Johnny. "Just watch. Listen. And learn."

Chapter Two
The Smelly Socks of Death

"Sorry that you got stuck beside me again," Dale said to Johnny.

Johnny had been right. Helping his dad pour gas into the tank of Coach Smith's car had made Johnny the last guy into the dressing room.

"Don't worry about it," Johnny said. "It has to happen to someone. Right, Tom?"

"Right," Tom said. Tom was on the other side of Dale. He was plugging his nose. "Remind me never to be late again."

Tom was the other center on the Timberwolves team. All of the players lived in a small town called Howling.

Tom had just joined the team this season. He used to live in a big city.

Tom lifted his thumb and finger away from his nose. "Nothing personal, Dale. This is the first time I've had to sit beside you. I'm not used to it."

"Nobody gets used to it," Dale said. "If you think it is bad sitting beside me, imagine what it is like to wear this stuff."

Dale lifted a pair of hockey socks out of his hockey bag.

"There they are," Johnny said sadly. He tried not to breathe through his nose. "The smelly socks of death."

"I get my mom to wash them every game," Dale said. "But then she throws them into my hockey bag and they get smelly again."

Dale didn't have to explain why. Inside the hockey bag were his smelly hockey gloves of death. His smelly shin pads of death. His smelly elbow pads of death. His smelly jockstrap of death. Everyone on the team agreed that Dale had the smelliest hockey equipment in the history of hockey.

"Got more of that stuff I used last week?" Johnny said. "You know, the heat rub."

"Sure," Dale said. He reached into his hockey bag. "Here."

It was a small tube of white ointment. It was supposed to be rubbed on sore muscles. It smelled like spearmint and peppermint. It was very strong.

"Thanks," Johnny said. He squeezed some heat rub out like toothpaste. He smeared it below his nose. The smell made his eyes water. But it was better than smelling the hockey socks of death. And the elbow pads of death. And especially the hockey gloves of death. "That's better."

"Me too," Tom said. Johnny handed him the tube. Tom rubbed some below his nose. "Thanks, Dale. That helps."

"No problem," Dale said. "Just remember to wipe it off before you play."

"Why?" Tom asked.

"Oh, boy," Dale said. "I thought you knew."

"Knew what?" Tom asked.

"That stuff stings when you get sweaty," Dale said. "It's just a lot worse if you don't wipe it off."

Chapter Three
It's about Teamwork

Johnny had a white smear around his lips. Stu skated beside him in the warm-ups before the start of the game. Stu Duncan was Johnny's best friend.

"Nice clown face," Stu said. "I hope you play better than a clown tonight. Especially if you want a chance at beating Tom in the goal-scoring race."

"It's not about scoring goals," Johnny said. "It's about teamwork."

"Amazing," Stu said.

"Not really," Johnny said. "I've always said it's about teamwork."

"No," Stu said. "Amazing that you sound truthful when you say that. It's me. Stu. Your best friend.

11

I know you want to win the goal-scoring race."

Johnny grinned. "You're right. I do."

Tom skated up to the two of them. He had a white line below his nose, just like Johnny.

"Nice clown face," Stu said.

Tom frowned. "I wiped as much off as I could. But it really stings when you sweat."

"Better than the smelly hockey socks of death," Johnny said.

"And the smelly hockey gloves of death," Stu said, "and the smelly jockstrap of death."

The three of them were skating a wide circle in their end. Their opponents were warming up on the other side of the ice. Tonight the Timberwolves were playing the Chinooks, a team from a town just down the road.

"Howling is a crazy small town," Tom said. "I thought nothing could surprise me about it anymore. But I was wrong."

"What surprises you?" Johnny asked.

"That no one has helped Dale get new equipment," Tom said. "He told me it smells because it's been handed down from brother to brother for the last fifteen years."

"Yeah," Johnny said. "He is brother number eight. No wonder his equipment is so smelly."

"Why doesn't his family get new equipment for him?" Tom asked.

"They don't have a lot of money," Stu said. "It's not a big deal. Not everyone can be rich like your family."

"It is a big deal if you have to smell it," Tom said. "It's like five skunks have sprayed him."

"Seven," Stu said. "I had to sit beside him last week. But we accept him the way he is."

"Yes," Johnny said. "That's because he is part of our team. And remember, Tom, it's all about teamwork."

"Amazing," Tom said. "You sounded very truthful when you said that. But I know you want to beat me in the goal-scoring race."

"Sure," Johnny said, "but I'm part of the team too. What's good for me is good for the team."

"Ha, ha," Tom said. "You need to work on sounding more truthful."

Before Tom could say anything else, the ref blew the whistle to start the game.

Chapter Four
The Race Gets Close

Three minutes were left in the game. The Chinooks were two men short. They were also losing by two goals. Everyone in the rink knew that the Timberwolves would win the game.

Coach Smith sent Johnny's line onto the ice. Johnny had already scored two goals. He needed just one more goal to tie Tom for goal-scoring leader in the league.

"This is great," Johnny said to Dale as they skated to the face-off circle. "Maybe we can each score a goal. I will be tied with Tom, and you can have your first goal of the season."

"That would be great," Dale said. "Some of the guys on the other team have been bugging me because I don't have a goal yet."

The face-off was in the Timberwolves' end.

Johnny lost the draw. The puck went to the Chinooks' defenseman. Johnny skated hard to block the shot. It bounced off his shin pad and past the defenseman. Past the Timberwolves' blue line.

It was easy for Dale to get to the puck first. There were only three Chinooks' skaters on the ice against the five Timberwolves skaters.

Dale raced forward with the puck. Johnny chased after him. They had a two-man breakaway!

"I'll go wide!" Johnny shouted to Dale. "Keep skating!"

The crowd cheered as they raced down the ice.

Now they were past the centerline. Then the Chinooks' blue line! Still just the two of them.

Johnny moved to the left. The Chinook goalie couldn't face both Johnny and Dale at the same time. The Chinook goalie stayed square to Dale.

Dale moved in close. He deked the goalie. The goalie fell. Dale had an open shot at the net.

He passed to Johnny.

Johnny was so surprised, he almost missed the puck. But the net was so open all he had to do was tap it in.

Goal!

Now Johnny was tied with Tommy in the goal-scoring race!

Johnny lifted his hands as the crowd cheered. Dale skated over and gave him a high five.

"Thanks," Johnny said to Dale. "Now let's get you a goal."

"Great," Dale said.

But now that a goal had been scored, one of the Chinook penalties ended. The Chinooks had four skaters on the ice. It was much harder to score.

The game ended before Dale had a chance to shoot on the net.

No goal for Dale. And only one game left for him to do it. That would be against the Gophers in a few days.

Chapter Five
Watch, Listen and Learn

With the game over, many of the parents walked into the dressing room. They congratulated the boys on their win against the Chinooks.

"Good game, you guys," Johnny's dad said. "Good work in the corners, Dale. Nice goals, Johnny and Tom. Now you're tied for the goal-scoring race, aren't you?"

"I don't know, Mr. Maverick," Tom said to Johnny's dad. "To me, it's all about teamwork."

"Amazing," Dad said. "You sounded very truthful when you said that. I almost believed you."

Then Dad sniffed and made a funny face. "Dale, do I smell the socks of death? Or did a little animal crawl in your hockey bag and die?"

19

"Haven't found dead animals in my hockey bag," Dale said. "But I do store it in the barn. Over Christmas vacation, the cat had kittens in it. They weren't litter trained."

"This town just gets better and better," Tom said. "Am I living in a bad dream?"

"Dale's got some heat rub you can put on your face," Johnny said to Dad. "That will help."

"No," Dad said, "heat rub hurts. I'll just go to the other side of the dressing room. Nothing personal, Dale."

"No problem," Dale said. "I understand. But I thought the mother might let the kittens die if I moved them from my hockey bag. They sure peed a lot for such little things."

Before Dad could move away, Coach Smith saw him.

"Hey!" Coach Smith said to Johnny's dad. "How's that gas guzzler of yours? We need to be nice to the world, you know."

"I wish I could drive a small car too," Dad said. "Four-wheel drives never get good gas mileage.

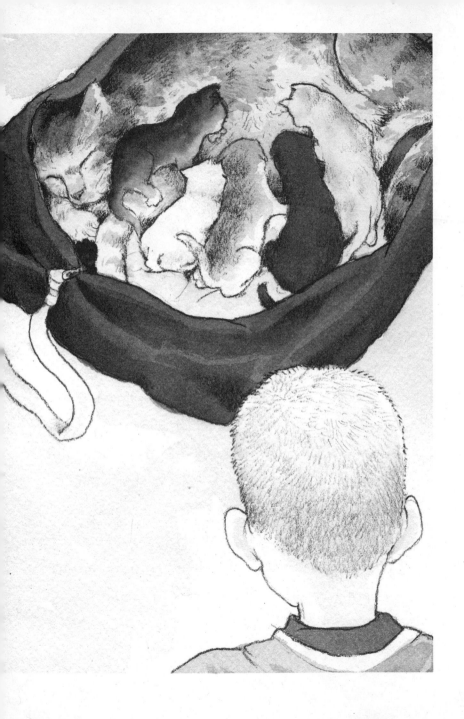

But with my job I can't afford to get stuck. I need something that can drive through and over anything."

"Well, let me tell you about my car," Coach Smith said. "Remember a few weeks ago how I told you I had a special computer tune-up? Now it doesn't use a drop of gas."

"Not a drop?" Johnny's dad said.

"Well, it uses some gas, of course," Coach Smith said, "but I'm getting at least seventy miles to the gallon."

"No way," Dad said. He saw that Johnny was listening. "How do you figure that?"

"Easy," Coach Smith said. "I keep track of how many miles I drive. I also keep track of how much gas it takes to fill the tank. In the last few weeks I went two hundred and ten miles and the car only used three gallons of gas. That's seventy miles to the gallon."

"Wow," Johnny's dad said, "that is amazing. Maybe you should tell someone at the newspaper about this. Everyone will want the kind of tune-up you just had. It might get you some extra business too."

"Good idea," Coach Smith said. "I just might do that."

Coach Smith walked away.

Johnny's dad smiled at Johnny.

"Remember," Dad said to Johnny. "Watch. Listen. And learn."

Chapter Six
Hallway Trouble

"Look at the *Howling Gazette*," Johnny said to Stu. Johnny was holding a newspaper. It was a week after their last game. They were standing in the library before school started. The library was one of their favorite places because they loved reading good books.

"Why should I look at the *Howling Gazette*?" Stu asked. "There's a new *Captain Underpants* book here."

Students went up and down the hallway outside the window. Johnny ignored them.

"Coach Smith wrote a letter to the paper about his car," Johnny said.

"What is there to write about?" Stu said. "It's not like he drives a Corvette. Or a cool 4x4 that can drive through and over anything."

"Really," Johnny said. "Here."

Johnny handed the newspaper to Stu. Stu started to read the article.

"I'm impressed," Johnny said. "Your lips don't move when you read."

"Ha, ha," Stu said. "Now be quiet."

Stu kept reading.

Seventy Miles to the Gallon!
Local Businessman Calls
Computer Tune-up a Success

Dear Editor,

I think it's a shame when the newspaper won't publish an amazing news story when it happens right in Howling. You probably won't even print this letter.

I've called three times to tell you about my computer tune-up. My car is getting seventy miles to the gallon. It's also wrong that your reporter would accuse me of lying about it. I am very careful with my calculations, and everyone in Howling knows I am a truthful man, especially in my insurance business on Main Street.

Yours truly, Jerry Smith

P.S. Anyone interested in helping the world with the same kind of tune-up can stop by my insurance business on Main Street. I would be happy to talk to them about my car or any of their insurance needs.

From the editor: As most of our readers know, Mr. Smith is the coach of the Howling Timberwolves. And our boys are having a good season. It's neck-to-neck between centers Johnny Maverick and Tom Morgan for leading goal scorers in the league. Come watch their last regular game of the season tomorrow night to see who wins. Go, boys, go!

"Seventy miles to the gallon," Stu said after he put the paper down. "That is amazing."

"What's amazing is that the editor put my name in at the end," Johnny said. "That's something to be proud of, wouldn't you say?"

"I also saw Tom Morgan's name."

"Right," Johnny said. "It's all about teamwork."

"Keep working on sounding truthful," Stu said. "Someday someone might believe you. But it won't ever be me."

Johnny wasn't listening. He had moved to the window.

"Stu," Johnny said, "that's Tom Morgan. He's carrying a bag of hockey equipment."

"So he didn't believe us!" Stu said. "We have to stop him."

Both of them ran out of the library. They ran down the hall. They reached Tom before he got to their classroom. They tackled him. All three of them went down in the hallway in a big pile.

27

"Are you guys crazy?" Tom asked, still lying on the floor with Johnny and Stu. "What is going on?"

"That's what I'd like to know too," a voice said.

The voice came from above them. It belonged to Mr. Wright.

Mr. Wright was the principal. And he did not look happy.

Chapter Seven
A First Time for Johnny

Tom spoke first. Tom and Stu and Johnny were sitting in Mr. Wright's office. A sign on his desk said, *The name is Mr. Wright, never Mr. Wrong. And don't forget it.*

"Do you have any idea how bad the smelly hockey socks of death are?" Tom asked Mr. Wright. "And the smelly hockey gloves of death? And the smelly elbow pads of death?"

"I do," Mr. Wright said. "When I was younger, I used to be the coach for Dale's first three brothers. I understand the equipment has been handed down for many more brothers. The hockey gear would be much worse now."

"Especially after the cat had a litter of kittens in it during the Christmas break," Johnny said. "Dale said the kittens peed a lot for being such little things."

Mr. Wright made a face.

"It's like five skunks sprayed it," Stu said.

"Seven," Tom said.

"I get the idea," Mr. Wright said, "but I still don't know why you ended up in the hallway like that."

"I talked to my dad about it," Tom said. "I explained that Dale's family doesn't have a lot of money. So my dad bought Dale some new equipment. I even put in part of my allowance. I brought it to school this morning to give to Dale."

"That's very kind," Mr. Wright said. "What a good idea. Dale could use the new equipment."

Tom crossed his arms and looked at Johnny and Stu. "That's what I told them. It's not my fault they tackled me in the hallway."

"Yes, it is," Johnny said. "Last night at practice we told you it was a bad idea. You should have listened."

"You should have listened to Johnny last night," Mr. Wright said to Tom. "It is a bad idea."

"But you just said it was very kind," Tom said to Mr. Wright. "You said it was a good idea. You said Dale could use the new equipment."

Mr. Wright pointed to the sign on his desk. *The name is Mr. Wright, never Mr. Wrong. And don't forget it.*

31

"It is kind," Mr. Wright said. "It is a good idea. Dale could use the new hockey gear. But it is a bad idea."

Mr. Wright looked at Johnny and Stu. "Did you tell Tom about the Christmas a few years ago?"

"We tried," Stu said, "but he didn't want to listen."

"Tom," Mr. Wright said, "one year some of the people in town got together and bought a bunch of toys for Dale's family. They left the toys on their doorstep on Christmas Eve. It was a good and kind idea, but it was a bad idea."

"I don't understand," Tom said.

"On Christmas morning, the people in Howling found all the toys on Main Street. Dale's father had driven over the toys again and again and again. All of us got the hint. We've left them alone ever since."

"I still don't understand," Tom said.

"Dale lives in a proud family," Mr. Wright said. "They don't want help. Have you noticed that Dale never complains about the smelly hockey gloves of death?"

Mr. Wright smiled. "Did I just say that phrase out loud? The smelly hockey gloves of death?"

"Yes," Tom said, "you did."

Mr. Wright frowned.

"Bad idea," Johnny said to Tom. "Sometimes Mr. Wright asks funny questions that he doesn't want answered."

Johnny looked at Mr. Wright. "Those were funny questions. Tom will learn not to answer your funny questions."

Mr. Wright began to smile again.

"You see, Tom," Mr. Wright said, "this is a small town. You are new to the town. As you get to know us, you will see that some good ideas are really bad ideas. Does that make sense?"

"Is that one of your funny questions you don't want answered?" Tom said.

Mr. Wright sighed.

"We wouldn't have tackled Tom if we could have reached him in time," Johnny said. "But we knew if Tom got into the classroom with the hockey equipment, Dale would never play hockey on the Timberwolves again. He'd think we felt sorry for him."

"I don't do this very often," Mr. Wright said. He stopped. "Actually, I've never done this before in all the times that Johnny Maverick has been in my office. So for the first time, I have to say Johnny is correct."

Mr. Wright stood. "You boys aren't in trouble. It would be wise not to let this conversation get outside of the office. Most of all, never let Dale or his father know about this."

"But how can we get him the new equipment?" Tom asked.

"Not my department," Mr. Wright said. Mr. Wright pointed to the sign on his desk. *The name is Mr. Wright, never Mr. Wrong. And don't forget it.* "I try to stick to questions I can answer."

Chapter Eight
Running on Empty

Johnny sat in the truck as Dad drove them to the rink.

"Now let's talk about tonight's game," Dad said. "It would be nice to win a trophy, but it's more important to feel good about how you won it."

"What do you mean?"

"People who score a lot of goals still can't do it without a team to help them all season," Dad said. "Just remember that."

Dad turned into the parking lot of the rink. He stopped beside Coach Smith's car.

"Not again," Johnny said.

"Again," Dad said.

"Don't you remember what happens when I'm late?"

Johnny said. He had already noticed the gas can in the back of the truck. "A couple of goals tonight and I might win a trophy. It would be nice if I didn't have to sit beside the smelly socks of death before the game."

"I need your help to watch for traffic," Dad said. "This is going great. Did you read Coach Smith's letter to the editor?"

Johnny got out of the big black 4x4 and walked around to his dad's side of the truck. "He already wrote the letter. What difference does it make if you get him up to eighty miles to the gallon?"

"That would be boring," Dad said. He reached into the back of the truck. He grabbed the small gas can. He tossed it to Johnny.

"Hey!" Johnny said. He jumped. He expected the gas can to be heavy. But it was empty.

His dad pulled a hose from the front of the truck.

"This is a siphon," Dad told Johnny. He held up the key to a car. "We will use it to take gas from Mr. Smith's tank and put it into the gas can."

"You are taking back all the gas you put into it?"

"Only a little at a time," Dad said. "I've been sneaking over to his house in the middle of the night for the last four days. I'd hate for the missing gas to show up on his fuel gauge."

Johnny thought about it. He was impressed.

"You really know how to mess with someone," Johnny said. "But I still don't understand how it will help us be good neighbors."

"If I tell you the plan," Dad answered, "you have to promise to keep it a secret."

"This should be good," Johnny said. "Tell me."

Dad told him the plan.

Johnny was right. The plan was good.

Chapter Nine
A Smelly Loser?

It was the middle of the third period against the out-of-town Gophers. Tom had scored one goal early in the first period. Johnny had scored no goals. So Tom was one goal ahead in the race for the trophy. Time was running out for Johnny.

Johnny got ready for a face-off on the right side in the Gopher's zone. Dale was his right winger. The Howling Timberwolves were up by three goals. Johnny knew he didn't have to worry about teamwork as much. He could try to score and the team probably wouldn't lose.

The ref dropped the puck. The Gophers' center pulled it back to the defenseman. The defenseman passed it up the boards to a winger. Dale chased the puck and got to the Gophers' winger.

Johnny raced to the net. He knew that Dale was good at fighting for the puck. Dale had given him a lot of good passes all year. When Johnny looked up, the puck was already coming toward him. Dale had beat the Gopher's winger and made another good pass!

Johnny got his stick on the puck. The Gophers' defenseman tried to knock it away, and the puck bounced to Johnny's skates. He kicked the puck ahead and managed to get it on his stick again.

The Gophers' defenseman tried knocking the puck away again. But missed.

Johnny had a clear shot. He saw a space between the goalie's pads. He shot the puck quickly. The defenseman knocked him down. But as Johnny was falling, he saw the puck go into the net!

Goal! The Timberwolves were up by four! He was tied with Tom for goal leader! Johnny jumped up with his arms in the air as the crowd cheered.

Dale skated to give Johnny a high five.

The Gophers' winger was skating beside Dale.

"Maybe you got the puck from me," the winger said, "but that's only because you smell so bad that it's hard to stay close and fight you for the puck."

"My center scored," Dale said. "That's what matters."

"Yeah," the winger said. "Good thing he can score. I heard you haven't had a goal all year. That makes you a smelly loser."

"Hey!" Johnny said.

"Ignore him," Dale said. "It doesn't bother me."

But Johnny could tell that Dale did feel bad. Johnny didn't think it was because the winger said Dale was smelly. Dale was used to that.

Johnny knew it was because Dale didn't have a goal yet. That had not bothered Johnny before. Dale always passed to him. Dale was always happy when Johnny scored goals for the team.

"Sure," Johnny said to Dale. "If it doesn't bother you,

then I will ignore him. Besides, we are winning by four goals. Teamwork, remember?"

Coach Smith waved at them to stay on the ice. Johnny and Dale skated back to center ice for the next face-off.

Chapter Ten
A Smelly Hug

This time Johnny won the draw. He slid the puck back to Stu Duncan on defense. Stu was better at squishing people into the boards than he was at skating with the puck. Stu knew this. He passed the puck back to Johnny.

Johnny was still excited from scoring a goal and tying Tom in the race. He was moving fast and turned sideways quickly with the puck. It fooled the center who was chasing him.

Johnny looked ahead. There were two defensemen between him and the net. If he didn't pass, it would not hurt the team. The Timberwolves were up by four goals.

Johnny decided to hang on to the puck. He raced toward the side of the ice. Maybe he could skate around the defenseman in front of him.

"Johnny!" Dale yelled for a pass.

The defenseman looked over at Dale for a split second. That was enough for Johnny to make his move. He beat the defenseman. The defenseman tried to sweep the puck off Johnny's stick, but the defenseman fell down.

Breakaway!

Now Johnny was inside the blue line. Out of the corner of his eye, he saw someone chasing him. He took a quick look.

Good, he told himself. It was only Dale.

The two of them had another two-man breakaway!

"Go wide!" Johnny yelled. If Dale did that, then the goalie would have more trouble. Because then the goalie would have to watch out for a pass from Johnny to Dale.

But if Johnny scored now, he would be one goal ahead of Tom. And time was running out in the game. It would be good to fool the goalie into watching out for Dale.

Dale went wide. The goalie moved a bit to Dale's side to cover for the pass. It opened up a hole on Johnny's side of the net.

Shoot! He told himself as he got closer to the net. Shoot!

Now the goalie shifted back to Johnny's side because it seemed like Johnny was going to shoot. There was less room now, but still enough for Johnny to score if he made a good shot.

Except now Dale was wide open, and there was much more room on Dale's side of the net.

So Johnny faked a shot but slid the puck over to Dale. The fake fooled the goalie and he went to his knees to block the shot. He was stuck on the ice. He could not move fast enough to cover the other side of the net.

The puck reached Dale's stick. Dale seemed surprised at the chance.

"Shoot!" Johnny yelled at him. "Shoot!"

Dale shot. He scored! He jumped high in the air.

"A goal!" he shouted. "A goal!"

Johnny skated toward him to give him a high five.

But Dale did not give Johnny a high five. Dale hugged Johnny. It was a smelly hug. A very smelly hug.

"You could be ahead of Tom in the scoring race," Dale said as he hugged Tom. "You should not have passed."

"We are a team," Johnny said. "That's why I passed."

Dale hugged him again. "Thank you!"

"Sure," Johnny said. He was happy he had passed to Dale.

But Johnny wasn't as happy that Dale was hugging him. Dale's hockey equipment smelled like it had been sprayed by seven skunks.

Something had to be done about the smelly hockey equipment of death.

Chapter Eleven
The Loud Crunch

After the game, Johnny's dad was waiting beside Johnny in the dressing room. Johnny just had to tie his shoes and he would be ready to leave. Johnny's dad had his nose plugged.

"Sorry," Dale said. He had all of his hockey equipment off. He was putting on his shirt.

"That's all right," Johnny's dad said with his nose plugged. "I know it is worse for you."

"Yes," Dale said, "but I scored a goal tonight. Did you see it?"

"I did," Johnny's dad said. "It was great."

Coach Smith stopped to talk to Johnny. "Good playing tonight."

"Thank you," Johnny said. He finished tying his shoes. "I liked your letter in the paper. It's amazing that your car gets seventy miles to the gallon."

Coach Smith groaned and shook his head. "Not anymore. Suddenly, I'm only getting twenty miles to the gallon. I can't figure out what is wrong."

"I'm sorry to hear that," Johnny's dad said to Coach Smith. "Especially after you bragged about it to everyone in town."

"I know," Coach Smith said. "That's the worst part."

"Dad," Johnny said. "I'm ready."

Johnny stood. He grabbed a bag of hockey equipment and hurried out of the dressing room. He walked with his dad to the end of the parking lot where the truck was parked beside Coach Smith's car.

"You seemed like you were in a hurry to leave the dressing room," Dad said.

"Yes," Johnny said. He walked around to his side of the truck with the hockey bag. He set it underneath the truck. "I was in a hurry."

"But we have to wait for Coach Smith," Dad said. "I explained that was part of the secret plan."

"Sure," Johnny said. He jumped up into his side of the truck.

Dad got into his side. He started the truck so they could stay warm. They waited for Coach Smith.

"It's going to be great when Coach Smith catches you taking gas out of his car," Johnny said.

"I think that it was great that you helped Dale score his first goal of the season," Dad said. "You could have scored an easy goal and beat Tom in the scoring race."

"I think Tom could have beaten me too," Johnny said. "Tom missed two wide-open nets in the last minute of the game."

"Strange, isn't it," Dad said. "Tom is usually so good. Instead the two of you ended up in a tie."

"Do you think it was strange?" Johnny said. "Tom won't admit it, but I think he missed on purpose."

"You mean because the team was up four goals and it didn't matter if he missed?"

"Yes," Johnny said.

"And because he's a good friend and saw that you gave Dale a chance to score?"

"Yes," Johnny said.

"I agree," Dad said. "I think Tom also knows it's nice to win a trophy, but it's more important how you win. Sharing it won't be bad, will it?"

Johnny didn't answer. He was looking back through the window. He saw that Dale and Dale's dad were running down the parking lot toward them.

"Back up, please," Johnny said.

"But we need to wait for Coach Smith," Dad said. "Remember?"

"I just need you to back up," Johnny said. "You don't have to leave the rink."

"Why?" Dad asked.

"So we can be good neighbors," Johnny said.

His dad began to back up. The truck tires hit something. Dad stepped on the brakes.

"What's that?" Dad said.

Dale and his dad were getting closer.

"This truck can go through and over anything," Johnny said. "Keep backing up. Hurry!"

"But we just hit something," Dad said.

"Remember you said you owe me for helping with Coach Smith?"

"Yes, but—"

"If you keep backing up," Johnny said, "we'll be even."

Dale and his dad were not far away now.

"Dad," Johnny said, "trust me. Hurry!"

Dad backed up. "What am I driving over? That was a big bump."

"Now forward," Johnny said. "Trust me. Hurry!"

Dad drove forward. There was another loud crunch.

"You don't have to drive over it again," Johnny said. "That should do it."

"It should do what?" Dad asked.

"Remember what you told me about your plan for Coach Smith?" Johnny said. "Watch. Listen. And learn."

Dale and Dale's dad reached the truck.

"Hey," Dale's dad yelled, "you just drove over my son's hockey bag!"

Chapter Twelve
Blame Dad

"This is my fault," Johnny said.

All of them were standing around the truck. Johnny and his dad. Dale and Dale's dad.

Johnny's dad had the flashlight from the truck. He shone it on the hockey bag.

Dale looked inside.

"Yes," Dale said, "it looks like my hockey stuff." He leaned down and sniffed. "Yes, that is my hockey stuff."

Dale's dad said, "You mean that *was* your hockey stuff."

Dale's hockey gear was smashed and broken.

"I took your bag out of the dressing room," Johnny said, "and I left behind my bag."

"You must have gotten the bags mixed up," Dale said. "We were trying to catch you before you left the rink."

"I am very sorry," Johnny said. "I put the bag on the ground where my dad didn't see it when he backed up."

"We can see it was your fault," Dale's dad said. He was angry. "What are you going to do about it? Dale needs hockey gear to play in the playoffs."

"Since it was my fault," Johnny said. "I will make sure I replace it. Would that be okay?"

"I guess," Dale's dad said, "as long as Dale has it by next game."

Dale's dad looked at Johnny's dad. "Next time, be more careful when you drive."

Dale's dad stomped away. "Come on, Dale. Let's go."

Dale shrugged and looked at Johnny. "Sorry," Dale said.

"No problem," Johnny said, "really. I'm happy to do it."

"At least you won't have to smell the hockey gloves of death ever again," Dale said.

"See?" Johnny said, "A person can always find a bright side."

Dale waved good-bye and followed his father.

Johnny and his dad got back into the truck to wait for Coach Smith.

"You switched bags on purpose," Dad said.

"I learn from the best," Johnny said. "Tom already has another bag of hockey equipment to give him."

Johnny saw Coach Smith step out of the rink. "Now it's your turn."

Dad hurried out of the truck. He released the gas cap to Coach Smith's car. He stuck the hose into the gas tank. He stuck the other end of the hose into the gas can.

Coach Smith walked up and saw Johnny's dad.

"Hey!" Coach Smith said. "What are you doing?"

"Nothing," Dad said.

"Nothing?" Coach Smith said. "That is a hose in my gas tank. Hey! You're stealing gas from me!"

"Hang on," Dad said. "It's gas I already put in there."

"What?" Coach Smith said. He was mad. "You better explain."

"We're friends," Dad said. "I was messing with you. For a while, I was putting gas into your car so it would look like you were getting a lot more miles for every gallon. Then I began taking it out so it would look like you were getting less."

"You might think that is funny," Coach Smith said. "I sure don't. Even if we are friends."

"I'm sorry," Dad said.

"Sorry?" Coach Smith was mad. "You know I don't like jokes. You should be more than sorry."

"Let me make it up to you," Dad said. "You told me that you're going to build a garage. I have lots of tools. If I help you build it, will that make us even?"

"I guess," Coach Smith said. "As long as you don't tell anyone about this."

"Deal," Dad said. He shook hands with Coach Smith.

Then Coach Smith saw the hockey bag and all the broken and smashed hockey gear. Coach Smith bent over to take a closer look.

"Yuck," Coach Smith said. "That smells horrible. Is it Dale's?"

"It *was* Dale's," Johnny said. "Now we have to throw it away and give him new equipment."

"Wonderful!" Coach Smith said. "How did this lucky accident happen?"

"It's a long story," Johnny said. "Let's just say we need to blame Dad."